CONTENTS

For Vikas,

Because of his appreciation, encouragement and support, I could become an author

PREFACE

This book is a work of love and passion. It is a humble effort to write for children who are always playing innovative games, doing some mischief or creating something new. Curious by nature, they have an intrinsic need to understand the world around them. What better means to tend to a fertile mind than through books, especially story books that attempt to fuel their imagination, answer some interesting 'Wh' questions and also entertain young readers?

If you have this book in your hands, please accept my heartfelt gratitude that you chose this book for your children or school library for them to read or for you to narrate.

Avi is a curious eight—year—old who lives with his parents and his best friend KIA—the 'Know It All' robot. Each day is a new day for him, filled with learning and discovery, as his best friend is always by his side, answering his endless questions. Let us try to wean our children away from screens and gadgets without compromising on the experiences they get from the tech world.

I hope you all enjoy reading and narrating the stories, as much as I have loved penning them for you.

Happy Story Time to you all.
Smriti Agarwal

ACKNOWLEDGEMENTS

My early memories of writing include letters and an account of my day's happenings in my diary. I was always an informal writer, as I would write a diary entry daily. My diary was my soulmate wherein I used to pour all my emotions into words and express myself. Whenever something bothered me or made me happy or hopeful, I would turn to my diary to find solace. It was my companion from the age of 10 till the age of 25.

The 1980s was a time for correspondence through letters. I used to write long letters to my cousins, maasis (aunts) and grandparents and they used to write back. This exchange taught me whatever I know of written communication, which helped me immensely in my career and life.

I developed an interest in reading and then writing because of my mom, late Mrs Neeru Agarwal. It was she who used to read me bedtime stories, she who insisted on buying books for us and cultivated a deep love for stories in all forms. My dear husband, Vikas was the one, other than my mom, who loved what I wrote and always had faith that I would become a beloved author one day. Thanks to his never–dying encouragement and support, I began to take myself and my writing seriously.

This book is the result of the enthusiasm of Renu Kaul Verma from Vitasta Publishing, who met me at an education conference and encouraged me to write a book. She was so keen that I took up the task instantly, as it was always my dream to be a published author. Renu, I love your warmth, your affection and your enthusiasm.

I sincerely thank the editorial team of Vitasta Publication and especially Saumya who improved the writing of this book many folds through their expertise and passion for books. Thank you, Rohit Gautam, for beautifully designing this book.

I have to thank my biggest critics, my siblings, Abhishek, Geetika and Pritish, who never take me seriously and always make it a point to let me know of my flaws. This awareness has helped me to make an effort to better myself at my craft, and it always will. Geetika and Pritish went through this book and gave me some pertinent feedback and insights, for which I am thankful to them.

The two-member team who made beautiful illustrations and designs for the book has my heartfelt thanks and they are Dinesh Agre and Suryakant Chavan. They patiently redid so many illustrations after my constant feedback and rejections, especially while creating Avi and KIA.

I will end my long gratitude list here and hope that I live up to the expectations of all my dear ones and most of all, You, the readers. If you enjoyed reading this book, do drop me an email, sharing your thoughts with me.

Lots of love and regards,
Smriti Agarwal
smritimohla@gmail.com

Avi's Game
And
French Fries
Avi was in his room working on something very intently.

Suddenly, he jumped up with joy and ran to the other room where KIA was sitting.

Avi had never been as excited in his eight years of life as he was now. Avi rushed to KIA and said, 'You know what I have made? My own game!'

KIA looked at him and corrected him, 'Not made, Avi, say you invented a new game.'

Avi looked at her, puzzled and asked, 'Invented? Meaning?'

KIA answered him, 'Avi, "invented" means to bring something new into the world which was not there before.'

Avi thought for a moment and then exclaimed, 'Like mom and dad invented me!'

KIA looked at him with a frown and said, 'No Avi, you were not invented, you were born.'

Avi looked at her and asked again, 'But you only said invention means to bring something into the world which was not there before. I know I was not there in the world and then mom and dad brought me into this world.'

'That is right, but you said it yourself that you were "brought into this world," so sorry my friend, but you were not invented,' KIA replied to Avi in a robotic tone.

Avi mocked her, 'How would you know? You are just five years old.'

KIA began to speak, but Avi cut her off with a frustrated sigh, 'I know your name already! Everyone knows you as KIA, the KNOW IT ALL Robot, who knows everything!'

KIA looked at him blankly.

Avi continued, 'Okay, so it is a discovery like in Discovery Channel!'

Everyday, there is a new discovery. Right, KIA?'

KIA sighed and said, 'No baba...not discovery! Invention! Discovery is different from invention. Discovery is to find or discover a thing which was there in the world in some form, but then either it was lost and found again, or a new thing was discovered about the existing thing.' KIA continued, 'Invention is something totally new, which was not there before.' Avi nodded his head seriously when he understood the difference.

'Oh, I see.'

'Okay, KIA, tell me were French fries discovered or invented?' 'French fries that you love so much were accidentally invented,' KIA replied.

'A Belgian cook...,' Avi then suddenly realised that he didn't know the meaning of Belgian.

'KIA what is the meaning of Belgian?' 'Belgium is another country, as you know India is a country,' KIA explained. 'In 1830, a Belgian cook accidentally invented French fries. Actually, he wanted to make potato stew for the

Belgian soldiers, when some potatoes fell in the frying pan in which he was heating the oil, instead of falling inside the stew pot,' said KIA, even as Avi listened with a lot of interest.

'The cook did not want to waste the oil and the potatoes and when the potatoes were fried, they emitted a delicious aroma, and the result was crisp fried potatoes. The soldiers were given the fried potatoes, and they loved the taste and asked the cook what these were and he answered in French, "Pommes frites," which means fried potatoes. Then it got famous by the name of "French Fries".'

'Oh! What an interesting story,' said Avi.

Avi was very excited to have learnt something new today.

KIA also reminded him, 'We learnt two things from this story:

Avi nodded in full agreement. Then he showed KIA the game he had invented. It was a board game with iron pawns, and he used a magnet beneath the board to move the pawns.

He tried to manoeuvre the pawns and they looked funny going all over the place. Avi would need practice to be able to control the magnetic movement. KIA and Avi had a hearty laugh and went to look for Avi's mom to show her the new invention.

Avi And His Blocks

It was Sunday and Avi was in his room sitting on the mat with all his blocks strewn all around. Avi was intently trying to make the tallest tower.

Avi was concentrating hard on the tower, feeling both happy and serious at the same time.

Just then, **KIA** entered his room and her beeping sound distracted him.

CRASH the tower fell

Avi and His Blocks

Avi was furious with KIA. 'Look what you did!' he shouted.
KIA looked at the scattered blocks. 'Oh, you were playing with Lego blocks? That is nice.' 'I was building a big, a very big tower but your beeping sound distracted me, KIA. Now look what happened,' Avi said with tears in his eyes.

'Why only a tower, Avi? Do you know that you can join two bricks with eight studs in twenty-four different ways, likewise six bricks can be combined in 102,981,500 ways?'

Avi was completely confused and puzzled at this information. He forgot all about his tower and wanted to know more.

'KIA, are you serious? How can we do that with the blocks?'
'Not any blocks, Avi, only Lego blocks.' Avi was now more curious than ever. He asked, 'What is the difference and why are these blocks called Lego blocks?'

KIA sat down and asked Avi to sit beside her and she started narrating the story of Lego.

Avi asked curiously, 'KIA, what is the meaning of "tend to his sheep?"'

'LEGO blocks originated in Denmark. There was a Danish carpenter called Ole Kirk Christiansen, who loved to make wooden toys when he used to tend to his sheep.'

'That is a nice question, Avi, you are paying attention to me,' KIA replied with a grin and continued, 'Tending sheep means he used to oversee the sheep when they grazed on the grass in the meadows. To pass his time sitting there, Christiansen used to carve little pieces of wood and shape them as whistles and toys. Later, he learnt the art of carpentry and worked on small jobs in his village, Billund. Then, he began making wooden toys in 1932. Two years later, he named his company LEGO after the Danish phrase, leg godt which means "play well" in English,' KIA explained.

Then KIA showed him a picture of Ole Kirk Christiansen.

'Wow!' Avi exclaimed. 'That is so great. But KIA, if Ole Kirk Christiansen only made wooden toys, then how and when were plastic Lego blocks created?'

KIA continued, 'The Leg Godt company made its first plastic block in 1949, but it was in 1958, eleven years later that this present design of blocks of stud-and-tube was manufactured. This design allowed the bricks/blocks to stay together and also be taken apart with a gentle pull or twist. Then in 1969, after Christiansen's death (he died in 1958), the blocks were made of a larger size, eight times larger than the original one. These blocks were good and safe for small children also to put together and play.

'Christiansen had a motto for his company and that was "only the best is good enough." His son Godtfred and his successors made sure of that. Avi was mesmerised with the story of the invention of Lego blocks. KIA reminded him, 'We learn from this story that we should strive to do our best because only the best is good enough. Hence, we should give our best to everything we do.

Do you agree with me, Avi?'
'Yes, KIA, I totally agree with you,' Avi said in full agreement.

Then KIA nudged him, 'Come let us try to make a very tall tower, like the one you were trying to make.' They both diligently kept one block over the other till the tower was really very tall. Avi ran out of his room and called his mom and dad to proudly show off his new creation.

Both mom and dad were very happy to see the tall tower that Avi and KIA had made. Avi silently thanked Ole Kirk Christiansen for giving the children of this world an amazing gift.

Avi
And The
National
Anthem
Avi was enjoying music and singing some of his favourite songs.

Jana-gana-mana-adhinayaka, jaya he

You are the ruler of minds of people, let the victory be with you

Bharata-bhagya-vidhata.
Punjab-Sindh-Gujarat-Maratha
Dravida-Utkala-Banga

The dispenser of the destiny of India—Punjab, Sindh, Gujarat, Maratha, Dravid, Orissa, Bengal

Vindhya-Himachala-Yamuna-Ganga
Uchchala-Jaladhi-taranga.

There are echoes in the hills of Vindhya, and the Himalayas and music is mingled in Yamuna, and Ganga which is chanted by foaming waves of the Indian Sea

Tava shubha name jage,
Tava shubha asisa mage,
Gahe tava jaya gatha,

Wake up listening to the auspicious name of yours and pray for your blessings. The savings of all the people is lying in your hands.

Jana-gana-mangala-dayaka jaya he
Bharata-bhagya-vidhata.
Jaya he, jaya he, jaya he, Jaya jaya jaya,
jaya he!

You are the one to impart well-being to the people, the dispenser of the destiny of India
May you get victory, victory, and victory for you!

Then suddenly he stopped singing his songs and started singing the Indian National Anthem. KIA saw him, puzzled, and waited for him to finish. Once he finished singing, she asked, 'Avi, why were you singing the national anthem just like that?

It is not a song that you can sing casually—anytime, anywhere. Haven't you learnt this in school?' Avi stood still and grimaced at KIA.

'I am not at school, KIA. Here at home, I can sing whatever I want to and when I want to.' KIA shook her round head disagreeing with him, 'No, you cannot. You must respect the national anthem and that is the reason that wherever you may be, you have to sing it in the proper way. There are rules to sing the national anthem. You must stand in a certain position and sing it in a specific manner to complete it within 52 seconds. Also, it should be played only when there is a purpose, and should be played only in the beginning or ending of an important event.'

Avi was stunned. He could not believe it and now he was curious to know more. 'KIA, sorry, I did not know all this. How did we begin singing the national anthem and when? Who wrote the national anthem and who composed the music and the tune for the national anthem?'

KIA shook her head again. 'Listen, Avi, sit here with me and let me tell you all about it. The Indian National Anthem was penned by...' Avi interrupted her, and said, 'What is the meaning of "penned"?' KIA explained, "to pen means to write. Our national anthem was written by Gurudev Rabindranath Tagore in Bengali language.'

'KIA, I do not understand the meaning of the words sung in the national anthem, also which language is it sung in now? I have just memorised the words, but I know nothing beyond that. Also, who was Gurudev Rabindranath Tagore?' Avi asked so many questions.

KIA laughed, 'Oh My God Avi! You have so

many questions. I will tell you about Gurudev some other time, but right now, let's learn about the national anthem.

'The first stanza of Gurudev Rabindranath Tagore's Bengali composition *Bharoto Bhagyo Bidhata* was performed as the national anthem for the first time by Tagore himself during a Congress meeting in Calcutta on 27 December 1911.

'It was adopted as our national anthem on 24 January 1950, when our constitution was made, just before 26 January 1950. The

language in which you sing is Hindi and you will understand it if you pay attention to the words, instead of just mugging it and repeating. Let me tell you about the words in Hindi with their English translation done by Gurudev.'

Then KIA showed Avi a picture of Rabindranath Tagore. Avi was very happy to know the meaning of the national anthem and seeing a picture of the great Rabindranath Tagore.

Both KIA and Avi felt immense pride in themselves and their country. KIA turned to Avi and said, 'We should always be proud of our country and strive to be good citizens of our nation.'

Avi And His Pencil

Avi was sharpening his pencils for school the next day, when the pencil point kept breaking making him both impatient and upset with the sharpener and the pencil.

Despite his impatience, Avi enjoyed collecting the pencil shavings. He continued sharpening his pencils, fascinated by the perfect spiral, snake-like shapes the shavings created.

Soon the pencil became very small, and Avi got sad. He went to KIA to borrow some pencils. KIA laughed and said, 'I do not use pencils Avi, as I do not write in notebooks or workbooks like you. I type and I have screens. You should not waste your pencils either as they are made up of wood, and we get wood from trees. Slowly, we will run out of trees. We must save them.'
Avi felt even more sad; he needed some pencils for school tomorrow. Just then his mom walked in and asked, 'Avi, have you arranged your bag for school?'

Avi replied with a small face, 'Yes, mamma, I have arranged everything, except the pencils. My pencils broke and now I do not have any.'

Mamma told him not to worry as she had some new pencils in her cupboard. She went to her room and brought three new pencils for Avi.

Mamma gave him a hug and told him to arrange his bag and go to sleep in ten minutes.

As mamma went out of the room, KIA asked him, 'Avi do you know what is inside the pencil?'

'Of course, "lead" duh!' Avi replied. KIA laughed at his reply. Avi looked at her and made a face, 'Why are you laughing? It is a fact.'

KIA replied, 'Let me tell you the facts. Way back in 1564, there was a big storm in England and a huge oak tree was uprooted. Beneath the roots, the local farmers found a black substance, which was mistaken to be "lead."

'It was amazing to write and draw with, but it always left black marks on the palms of the hand. To solve this problem, the farmer community tied string on the lead to keep the hands from getting messy.'

Avi listened intently and asked, 'Oh, I see! 1564? How many years ago was this?'

'Around 550 years ago,'

KIA replied. '500 years!' Avi exclaimed. 'Yes,' KIA continued, 'then in 1683, that is 140 years after the storm, a man named J Pettus created the first wooden pencil by slicing a small wooden piece length wise, hollowing out the middle and filling a rod of the black lead inside it. Then he glued the two pieces of wood which he had cut.'

KIA showed Avi the picture of probably the first pencil on her screen. 'See, Avi, this is the oldest pencil in the world, found in a timbered house built in 1630.' (Image: Faber-Castell)

'After that in 1779, a scientist discovered that actually it was not lead, but a form of carbon. He named this substance graphite which was an adapted word from the Greek word *graphein* which meant "to write." So, my dear Avi, it is not lead but graphite which is there inside your pencil.'

Avi looked at his pencils carefully as if trying to see the graphite inside. Suddenly, he had a thought. He asked KIA, 'Why do we have HB bonded lead written on my pencil?' KIA explained, 'Avi, HB means Hard Black. Pencils have different numbers and letters on them which denote the hardness of the graphite inside. The softer the graphite filling inside a pencil, the darker it writes, like 2B, 4B, i., Those pencils are used by artists to draw and sketch.'

Mamma came in the room again and got upset to see Avi still sitting with KIA with his pencils in hand and that he had neither sharpened them, nor arranged his bag for school the next day.

Avi hurried to his room and within minutes had finished his chores and was in his bed, thinking about the pencil and how he would now try to sharpen them and waste them less as they are made of wood and graphite and wood comes from trees.
'If we need to save trees, we must take care of our papers and pencils,' he thought while dozing off.

Avi And The Solar System

Avi was very busy. He did not have time to play or talk to KIA today. He had a school project on 'Solar System' which he had to complete and submit to his class teacher the next day.

He was diligently making big and small balls from his clay dough according to the size and colour of the planets. He made eight balls of various colours and sizes, when mamma walked in and said, 'Avi, there are nine planets. Why have you made only eight?'

KIA was sitting nearby reading a book. She looked at mamma and corrected her, 'No mamma, there are only eight planets.' Mamma turned to look at her and said, 'Okay, Ms KIA, the Know It All, let us count. Mars, Mercury, Earth, Jupiter, Saturn, Neptune, Venus, Uranus and Pluto. Nine!'

KIA corrected her again, 'Mamma, on 24 August 2006, it was declared that Pluto is a dwarf planet like Ceres. It does not fit the definition of a planet like the other eight in clearing the debris or asteroids to orbit around the sun.'

Mamma was confused and she checked this fact through the search engine on her mobile phone. She realised that KIA was indeed correct again as always. She smiled, 'Hail KIA! You are right.'

Avi spoke up: 'Yes, mamma, the teacher also taught us in class that there are eight main planets, and that Pluto is a dwarf planet.' Avi was curious now. He asked, 'KIA, who was the first astronaut

who went to space? Does a space suit help them to breathe? How do they survive in space for so many days?'

KIA shook her head and laughed, 'As always Avi, you have so many questions. Okay, let me answer them, one by one. The first astronaut in the world who explored space was Yuri Gagarin of the Soviet Union. His vehicle, Vostok 1 circled Earth at a speed of 27, 400 kilometres per hour with the flight lasting 108 minutes. Then Neil Alden Armstrong , an American astronaut, was the first man ever to land on the moon in 1969.' KIA explained everything to Avi and showed him a picture of the astronaut on her monitor.

Avi thought for a moment and asked, 'KIA, is there no Indian astronaut who has gone into space?'

KIA replied, 'Mr Rakesh Sharma was the first vyomanaut who went into space, but he could not land on the moon.'

Avi started laughing and said, 'KIA it's an astronaut not v-yo-ma-naut.'

KIA sighed and replied to Avi, 'Vyomanaut is an Indian astronaut. Vyoman, in Sanskrit language means the "sky or space," and that's why an Indian astronaut is called a vyomanaut to distinguish him or her from an American astronaut.'

'Oh! I see,' replied Avi. 'But wait a minute, you said her? Are girls or women also astronauts?' Avi asked in surprise. KIA said, 'Of course! Kalpana Chawla was the first India-born American astronaut to go to space.' Then KIA showed Avi a picture of Kalpana Chawla.

'Ok, now about your other questions Avi, yes, a space suit is essential for all astronauts, and it is made up of multiple parts. Space suits help astronauts in many ways. It protects astronauts from getting too hot or cold. Space suits also give astronauts oxygen to breathe while they are working in space. The suits can also hold water to drink. Now, I think it is better that you get back to your project or else it will not be completed on time.'

Avi realised that it was getting late and that soon it would be time for dinner, so he got back to his project, saying, 'I will also be a vyomanaut when I grow up.'

KIA said, 'Whatever you want to do or be in life, put in a lot of hard work and focus on your mission, Avi. Study well and prepare well, then you can be anything you want to be.'

Avi replied, 'KIA, I will surely do that.' And he got busy with his project.

Avi
And
Global
Warming
Avi came
home from school,
threw his bag on the
bed and sat down, feeling
tired and exhausted.
'Oh! I am feeling so
hot. What's wrong with
the weather? It is
just April.'

KIA came and sat down next to him. 'I know, even I am burning up. It is all because of global warming, Avi.'

'Global warming! What is that?' Avi looked at her and asked in surprise.

Just then mamma came in and asked Avi to wash his hands and change his school uniform, and then come to the dining room to have his lunch. Avi did as mamma told him. After washing his hands and changing his clothes, he sat down at the dining table for lunch.

On the dining table, Avi asked KIA again, 'What is global warming? What does that have to do with the weather and the climate?' KIA explained, 'Avi, actually when we use a lot of resources for energy like coal, gas, wood, etc., they release a gas called carbon dioxide.' Avi interrupted with his mouth full of food, 'Carbon dioxide is what we also breathe out. My teacher had taught us that we breathe in oxygen and breathe out carbon dioxide.'

'Yes Avi, that is correct,' said KIA.
'Now, tell me where do we get oxygen from?'
'I know this. Trees and plants,' Avi replied enthusiastically.

'That is absolutely correct, Avi. But as we humans are increasing population on Earth, we are cutting down trees to make space for houses, businesses, and industries. Oxygen levels are decreasing as the use of various resources increases, leading to a rise in carbon dioxide. Vehicles burn petrol or diesel for movement, releasing carbon dioxide into the atmosphere. Additionally, all humans exhale carbon dioxide, contributing to the ever-increasing carbon footprint on Earth.

'You just told me that we breathe in oxygen which plants give us, but do you also know that plants need the carbon dioxide we breathe out to make their food? Now when trees and plants are reduced in such extremely large quantities, oxygen is less and carbon dioxide which we are constantly releasing in the air is in excess.

'This excess carbon dioxide left in the Earth's atmosphere traps heat, making the Earth warmer than it was fifty years back. This is global warming which is now even causing the Earth's glaciers to melt.'

Avi looked at KIA in disbelief and said, 'Haw! KIA, this is dangerous! Isn't it? What do we do about this? Is this the reason for the untimely rains during the winters, cloudbursts and storms in summers?'

Mamma interrupted and told Avi to stop talking and first finish his lunch. Avi then washed his hands and mouth, and came back to sit with KIA, curious to know what we could do to stop global warming.

Avi and KIA were sitting on the living room couch, when KIA said, 'Avi, you are right. The unpredictable weather and out-of-season showers of rain, tornados, and calamities are all because of climate change due to global warming.' Avi was speechless.

KIA continued, 'We need to reduce wastage of natural resources, our carbon footprint and excess use of vehicles and fuels to solve the problem.' Avi got sad and asked, 'How is that possible, KIA? Everywhere we see buildings, construction sites and thousands of vehicles on the road.'

KIA cheered him by saying, 'It is not like this, Avi. The world is waking up to this concern and now we have electric vehicles and Sustainable Development Goals set by the United Nation to work towards a sustainable world for the coming generations. Together, we need to be mindful and use carpools, cycles and public transport instead of individual vehicles to commute. We also need to stop deforestation and plant more trees. Each of us has to do their bit.'

Avi smiled and said, 'Yes, KIA we can together reverse the effects and be mindful so that we can stop this dangerous situation from becoming worse. Electric vehicles or EVs, like electric cars and scooters are a new concept and I am sure that with time, more people will use them instead of petrol or diesel cars.'

KIA laughed and lovingly ruffled Avi's hair. 'You know Avi, the first EV was invented and showcased in 1835 by a British inventor called Robert Anderson. His vehicle used a disposable battery powered by crude oil to turn the wheels. At the same time, others in different countries were also trying to make an electric vehicle.

'Then, in the 1860s, a French physicist by the name of Gaston Plante invented the first rechargeable lead-acid battery—a huge breakthrough for electric mobility. However, it wasn't until the late 1880s that these inventions (batteries and electric motors) were put together by electric mobility pioneer William Morrison to create the first "practical" EV.

'See, it is not an invention.' Then KIA showed Avi the first electric car of the nineteenth century.

'Woah! Slow down KIA,' Avi said, his head spinning with so much information.

KIA laughed and continued, 'In the early twentieth century, there were more electric vehicles than petrol vehicles on American roads. But after that, for many years, gasoline cars became more popular, and now with time and advanced lithium batteries, EVs are making a big comeback. Today, it is considered as the most sensible way to commute.'

Avi was very surprised and also extremely happy that finally people were doing something to save the Earth. He now believed that everyone will have to contribute to make Earth a liveable planet, not only for now but for the coming generations too.

Avi and KIA went for a walk around the neighbourhood. Avi was walking with KIA, but he was not listening to a word that she was saying.

KIA soon realised this and asked Avi to tell her what was bothering him. Avi explained, 'KIA, the air does not feel fresh and there is so much noise here, hurting my ears. I do not know what is wrong, but I am not enjoying the walk.'

KIA said, 'I see. Avi, do you know what pollution is?'
'Of course, I do KIA. There are various kinds of pollution: land, air, and water. My teacher has taught us about pollution. But I would love to know more. Tell me more about pollution, KIA.'

KIA explained to him that apart from land, air and water, there is another type of pollution called noise pollution.

'We need to create a lot of awareness to restrain noise pollution. We are surrounded by loud noises like loud music from speakers, noise from construction sites and electrical appliances. All these affect our mental and physical health in an adverse manner, meaning that is harmful for us.'
'Yes! You are absolutely right, KIA. Yesterday only when I was coming back from the market, someone was playing loud music. Oh my, it was horrible! And don't talk about these construction sites. But KIA, how can we control noise pollution?' asked Avi.

'Avi dear, we need to take cautious steps and be mindful to turn off appliances like television, computers, music systems, etc., when not in use and when we are using them also, we should use them at a lower volume which does not hurt our ears or disturb others.' Avi nodded.

'Loudspeakers and DJ (Disc Jockey) speakers during events, functions and festivals need to be within the prescribed decibel levels but during celebrations, people forget all about the environment and the law and go above a certain decibel level.'

Avi asked, 'Decibel level! What is that? How can we measure the loudness of any sound?'
'Nice question, Avi,' KIA said.

'The sound-level meter is a device which is used for measuring the intensity of noise, music, and other sounds. A typical meter consists of a microphone for picking up the sound and converting it into an electrical signal, followed by electronic circuitry for operating on this signal so that the desired characteristics can be measured. The indicating device is usually a meter calibrated (adjust or fine-tune) to read the sound level in decibels (dB; a logarithmic unit used to measure the sound intensity). Threshold of hearing is about zero decibels for the average young listener, and threshold of pain (extremely loud sounds) is around 120 decibels, representing a power 1,000,000,000,000 (or 1012) times greater than zero decibels.'

Avi thought for a moment and replied, 'But if I am listening to music and mamma is grinding something in the food processor, we are doing that in our own home and that should be fine, isn't it?'

KIA explained to him, 'Let us think about it in another way. Now, imagine every household is making some noise through electrical appliances, music, children bursting crackers, and by repair, or construction, etc., in a neighbourhood. Collectively, how much noise pollution will that be? It will create havoc all around the neighbourhood. Hence, we need to be mindful of the volume of noise we are creating.'

'Oh! yes,' Avi said thoughtfully.

KIA continued, 'Hence, my dear, Avi, we should also plan and keep generators and washing machines in an open area or backyard, where it does not disturb people in their bedrooms while they are sleeping, reading or when children are studying. Until the time each one of us mindfully does not curb the noise we create and lower the decibel levels around us, we will always be exposed to mental and physical health risks.'

Avi was playing in the garden, flying his kite and enjoying. While running, he could smell something pungent. He stopped playing and covered his nose. Oh God! It was such a foul smell. He went ahead to find the source of the bad smell and realised that there was a stack of garbage near the park.

The garbage had not been removed for days and was spreading this foul odour. There were flies and mosquitoes all around. He quickly moved away from the spot and ran back home.

KIA met him at the door. 'Slow down, Avi, why are you running? What happened?' she asked. Avi wriggled his nose and told her about the garbage dump he saw. KIA gave him a glass of water and made him sit on the chair. KIA told him that the garden was a beautiful place some years back, with fresh air and blooming flowers. There was a sweet fragrance all around and people loved going there for a morning walk. But that was not happening now because of a lot of litter and garbage around the garden.

'KIA, where does so much garbage come from?' Avi asked, sipping his water.
KIA replied, 'Avi, see, when we buy more than we want, we create more waste. There is a big difference between "needs" and "wants".'

Avi was perplexed and said, 'Needs and wants are the same things, KIA. What's the difference?' KIA shook her head and said, 'No, Avi. Needs are when one requires them to fulfil something important in life such as food, electricity, etc., but wants are things you buy to fulfil a desire. When one buys things that are needed, it is fine but wants must be minimal and well thought of.

'I will give you an example, you have many toys to play with, but still you buy one more toy, even when you don't need it.

'That is a want, but when your shoes are worn out and you buy a pair of shoes, that is your need. We need to reduce our wants. One must refuse to buy things that are not needed.

'Reduce and refuse are two important 'R's to add in the three 'R's of waste management. Avi, it is sad the way people keep buying electronic gadgets, just for a new model or do not restrict the use of plastic and polyethene, which are piling up as garbage mountains on earth.' Avi asked curiously, 'What can we do to save the earth from all the garbage?'

KIA answered, 'Apart from the two 'R's I told you about, people need to separate the dry waste, recyclable waste and make vermicompost out of the wet waste. There is a lot we can do to save the environment and our planet. Only, there should be a will to do so.' Avi said, 'My teacher also told me about the 5 'R's of waste management to save the Earth, but I do not remember what those '5 R's' are, KIA. Can you remind me.'

KIA then showed him the '5 R's'. They both gave a high five to each other and promised to save the Earth and spread this message to others.

KIA showed him the '5 R's'.

Avi promised KIA that he will:

'Reduce' wants.

'Refuse' things which are not eco-friendly.

'Reuse' things that can be used again and not buy new ones.

'Recycle' whatever can be recycled.

'Repair' old items, instead of discarding them.